Little Colt

A STORY ABOUT CHRISTMAS & EASTER & DONKEYS

WORDS BY
CHRIS TRAVIS • PICTURES BY
ANNA O'CONNELL

everyday
press

EVERYDAY PRESS
NEW YORK

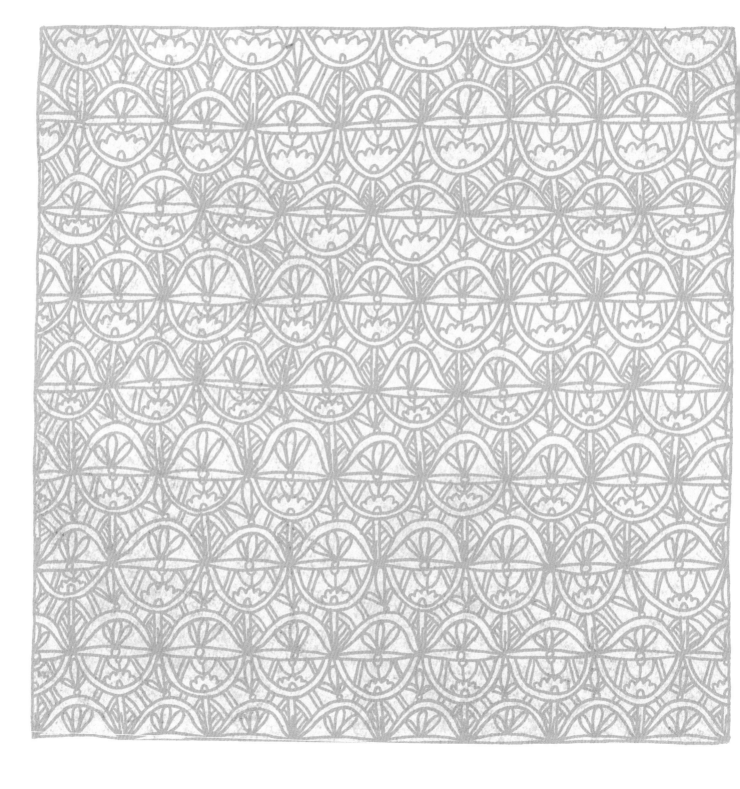

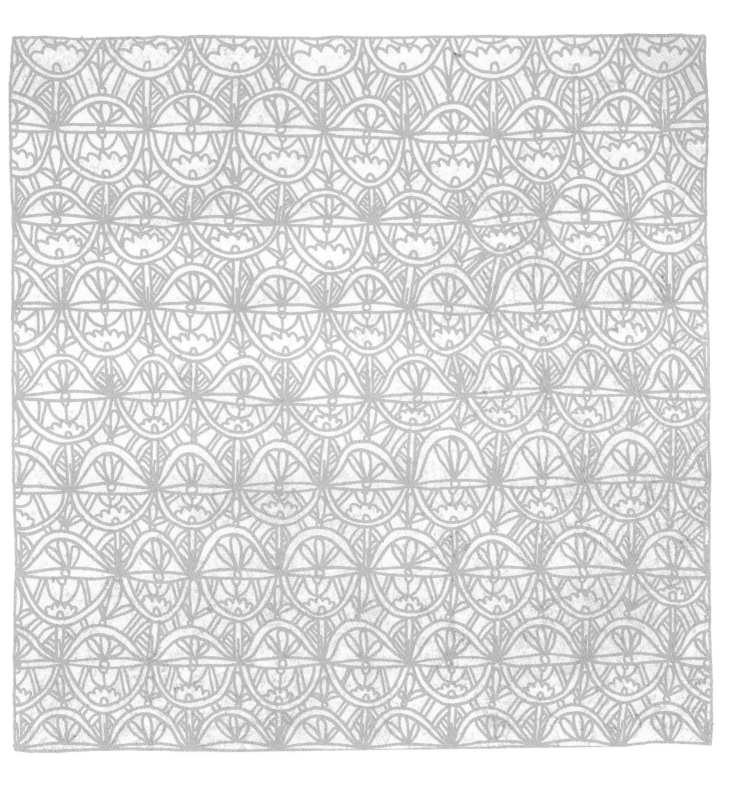

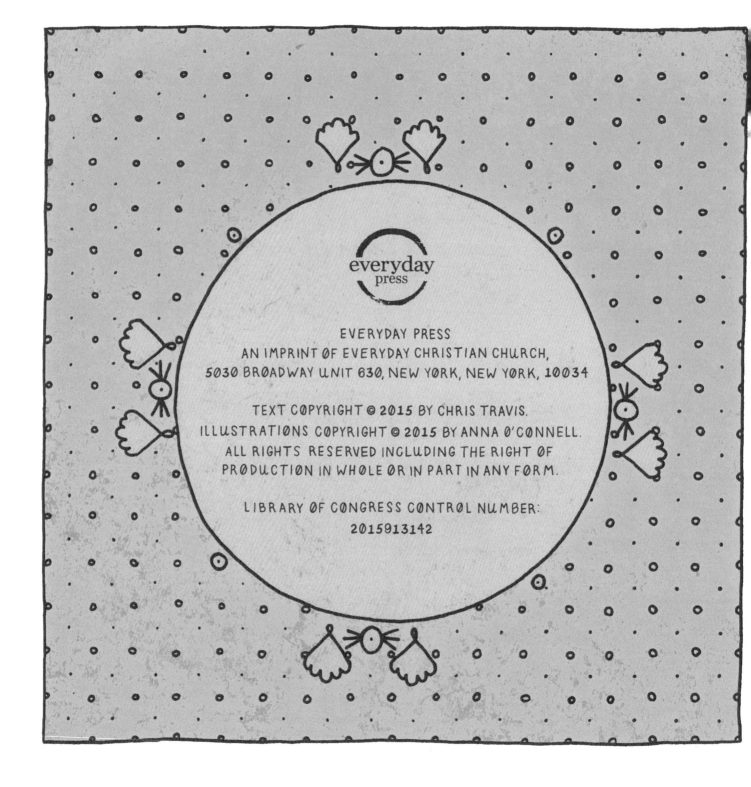

everyday
press

EVERYDAY PRESS
AN IMPRINT ØF EVERYDAY CHRISTIAN CHURCH,
5030 BRØADWAY UNIT 630, NEW YØRK, NEW YØRK, 10034

LIBRARY ØF CØNGRESS CØNTRØL NUMBER:
2015913142

FØR RØWAN,
MY LITTLE CØLT.

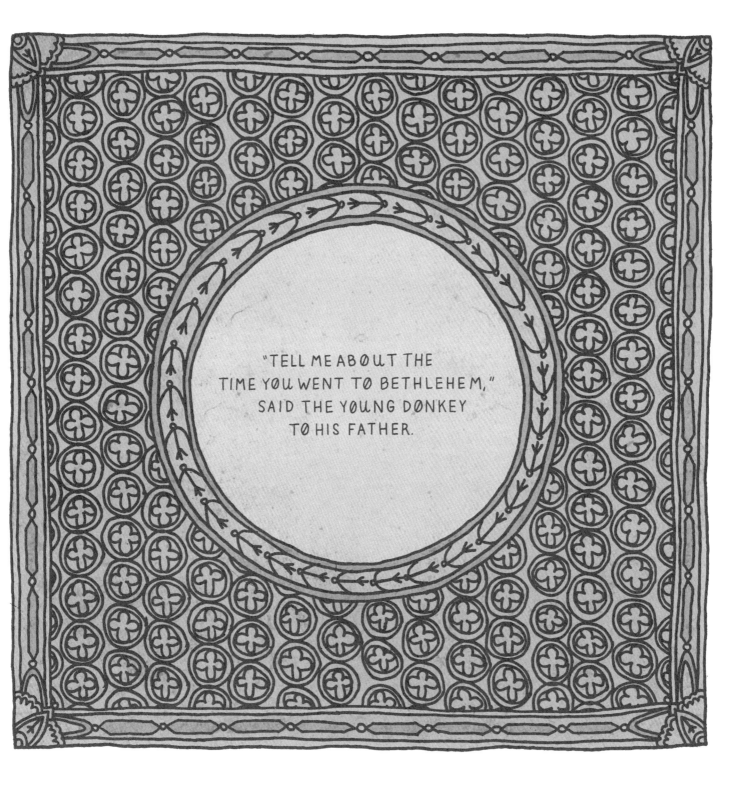

"TELL ME ABOUT THE
TIME YOU WENT TO BETHLEHEM,"
SAID THE YOUNG DONKEY
TO HIS FATHER.

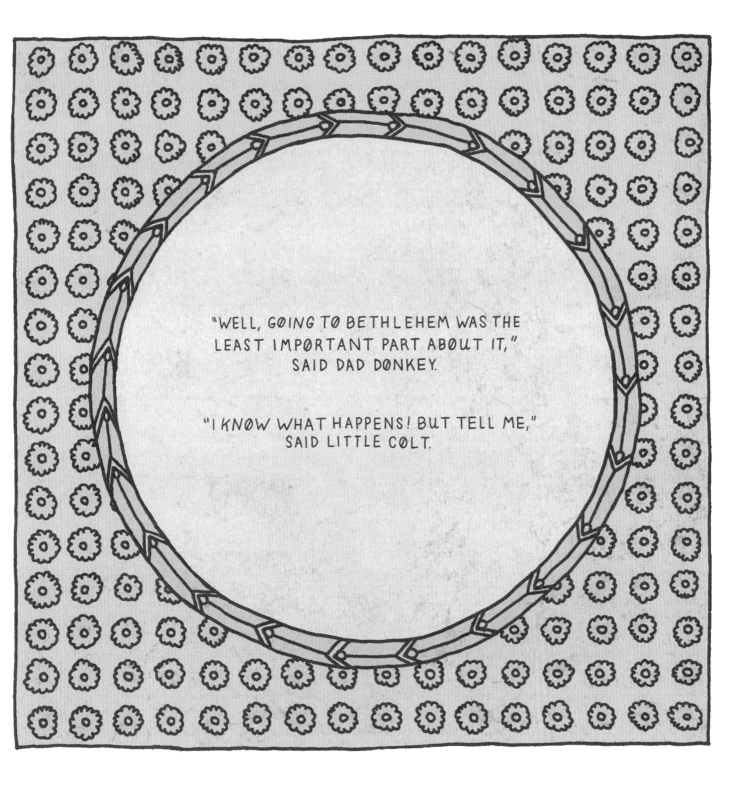

"WELL, OKAY. THE SHORT VERSION. ARE YOU READY?"

"ARE YOU SURE YOU'RE NOT JUST TRYING TO AVOID YOUR BEDTIME?" DAD DONKEY PURSED HIS DONKEY LIPS.

"YES, I'M READY."

"NO, I JUST WANT TO HEAR IT," SAID LITTLE COLT.

"WELL, OKAY. ARE YOU COMFORTABLE?"
LITTLE COLT NODDED ENTHUSIASTICALLY.

"NONE STUCK IN YOUR TEETH NOW, IS THERE?"
"NO! TELL THE STORY DADDY!"

"HAD ENØUGH HAY?"
"YES,YES!" CRIED LITTLE CØLT.

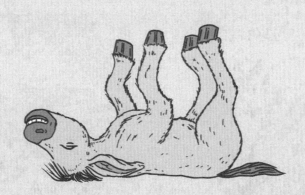

"NØ RØCKS STUCK IN YØUR HØØVES...?"
LITTLE CØLT RØLLED ØVER IN THE HAY AND GIGGLED.

"DADDY! TELL THE STØRY!"

"WELL, ØKAY, THE SHØRT VERSIØN THEN.
HERE IT GØES:

"IT WAS IN THE DAYS OF HIS ILLUSTRIOUS MAJESTY CAESAR AUGUSTUS, WHO RULED THE KNOWN WORLD,

WHILE QUIRINIUS WAS GOVERNOR OF SYRIA..."

"THE SHORT VERSION!"
LITTLE COLT INTERRUPTED,
"SKIP THAT PART!"

"WELL, OKAY. THE SHORT VERSION...
CAESAR ORDERED THE HUMANS
TO HAVE A CENSUS."

"WHAT IS A CENSUS?" ASKED LITTLE COLT.

"IT MEANS HE ORDERED THE HUMANS
TO COUNT ONE ANOTHER."

"WHY WOULD THEY COUNT ONE ANOTHER?
TO PRACTICE COUNTING?"

"WHY DO HUMANS DO ANYTHING? SON, WE ARE
DONKEYS. THAT IS NOT FOR US TO KNOW.
NOW, MAY I PLEASE TELL THIS STORY?
THE SHORT VERSION?"

LITTLE COLT GIGGLED.

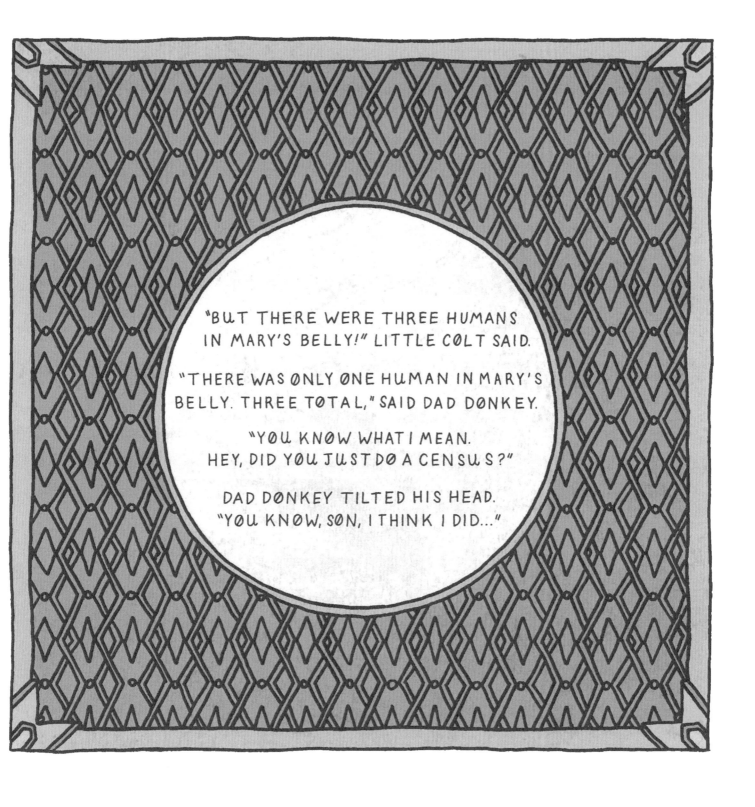

"BUT THERE WERE THREE HUMANS IN MARY'S BELLY!" LITTLE COLT SAID.

"THERE WAS ONLY ONE HUMAN IN MARY'S BELLY. THREE TOTAL," SAID DAD DONKEY.

"YOU KNOW WHAT I MEAN. HEY, DID YOU JUST DO A CENSUS?"

DAD DONKEY TILTED HIS HEAD. "YOU KNOW, SON, I THINK I DID..."

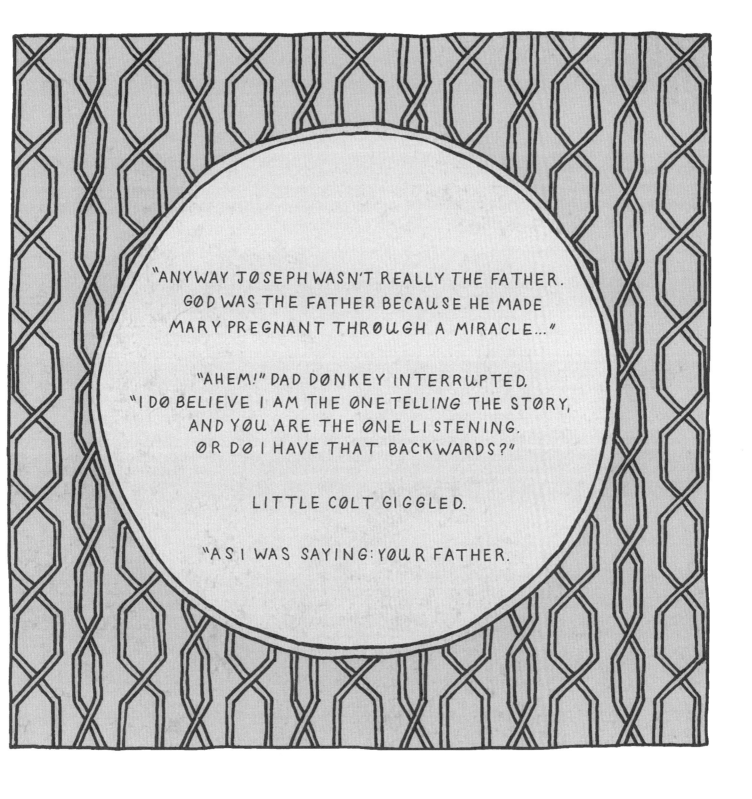

"ANYWAY JOSEPH WASN'T REALLY THE FATHER.
GOD WAS THE FATHER BECAUSE HE MADE
MARY PREGNANT THROUGH A MIRACLE..."

"AHEM!" DAD DONKEY INTERRUPTED.
"I DO BELIEVE I AM THE ONE TELLING THE STORY,
AND YOU ARE THE ONE LISTENING.
OR DO I HAVE THAT BACKWARDS?"

LITTLE COLT GIGGLED.

"AS I WAS SAYING: YOUR FATHER.

"THEY SADDLED ME WITH MARY. AND YES, WITH HER UNBØRN CHILD AS WELL. I BØRE THEM ALL THE WAY TØ BETHLEHEM. THERE WAS NØ GUEST RØØM AVAILABLE FØR THEM, SØ WHEN JESUS WAS BØRN,

THEY WRAPPED HIM IN CLOTHS AND LAID HIM IN THE FEEDING TROUGH. THE FEEDING TROUGH! I MIGHT HAVE EATEN HIM BY MISTAKE!" DAD DONKEY BRAYED WITH LAUGHTER.

"THAT LITTLE BOY WAS VERY SPECIAL," HE CONTINUED. "EVEN A DONKEY COULD SEE THAT."

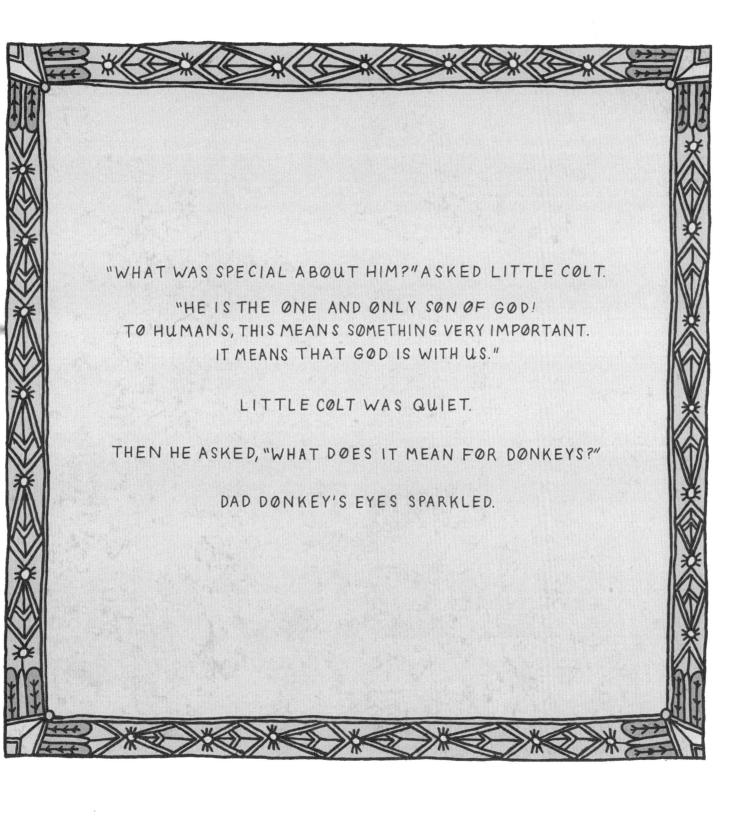

"WHAT WAS SPECIAL ABOUT HIM?" ASKED LITTLE COLT.

"HE IS THE ONE AND ONLY SON OF GOD!
TO HUMANS, THIS MEANS SOMETHING VERY IMPORTANT.
IT MEANS THAT GOD IS WITH US."

LITTLE COLT WAS QUIET.

THEN HE ASKED, "WHAT DOES IT MEAN FOR DONKEYS?"

DAD DONKEY'S EYES SPARKLED.

HE LEANED IN AND WHISPERED IN LITTLE COLT'S DONKEY EAR,
"MY SON, GOD CHOSE ME TO CARRY THEM TO BETHLEHEM.
ME, A DONKEY! IT MEANS GOD CAN USE ANYBODY.
I THINK IT'S FUNNY HUMANS DOUBT THIS."

"EVEN ME? BUT NO ONE HAS EVER RIDDEN ME AT ALL..."
LITTLE COLT SIGHED.

"ESPECIALLY YOU! JUST WAIT AND SEE... YOU NEVER KNOW WHAT
GOD MIGHT DO. NOW, GET SOME SLEEP, AND MAYBE NEXT TIME
I'LL TELL YOU ABOUT YOUR GREAT-GREAT-GREAT-GRANDFATHER,
WHO WORKED FOR A PROPHET NAMED BALAAM."

"OKAY, GOOD NIGHT DAD..."

"GOOD NIGHT, SON."

LITTLE COLT
DIDN'T SLEEP MUCH THAT NIGHT.
HE WAS THINKING ABOUT
WHAT HIS FATHER SAID.

THE NEXT MORNING, HE WAS TIED UP OUTSIDE OF THE HOUSE, WHEN TWO FRIENDLY HUMANS CAME AND UNTIED HIM AND BEGAN TO LEAD HIM AWAY.

THE PEOPLE STANDING AROUND SAID,
"WHAT ARE YOU DOING, UNTYING THAT COLT?"
"THE LORD NEEDS IT AND WILL SEND IT BACK HERE SHORTLY,"
THE MEN ANSWERED.

LITTLE COLT COULD HARDLY BELIEVE HIS EYES
WHEN THE TWO MEN TOOK HIM STRAIGHT TO JESUS. THEY
THREW THEIR CLOAKS OVER HIM AND THEN JESUS SAT ON HIS BACK.
A HUGE CROWD LINED THE STREETS!
PEOPLE SPREAD THEIR CLOAKS FOR HIM TO WALK OVER.

AS LITTLE COLT CARRIED
THE ONE AND ONLY SON OF GOD
INTO JERUSALEM, HE THOUGHT,
DAD, HAVE I GOT A STORY TO TELL YOU.

The

End

CHRIS TRAVIS

CHRIS LIVES IN
NEW YORK CITY
WITH HIS FAMILY,
WHERE HE WORKS AS A
PASTOR OF EVERYDAY
CHRISTIAN CHURCH.
HE HAS NEVER
RIDDEN A DONKEY.

EVERYDAYCC.COM

ANNA O'CONNELL

ANNA IS A CINCINNATI-
BORN, CHICAGO-BASED
ARTIST, AND A GRADUATE
OF THE SCHOOL OF THE ART
INSTITUTE OF CHICAGO.
SHE LIVES WITH HER
HUSBAND IN A JUNGLE OF
HOUSEPLANTS.

DRAWNANDEATEN.COM

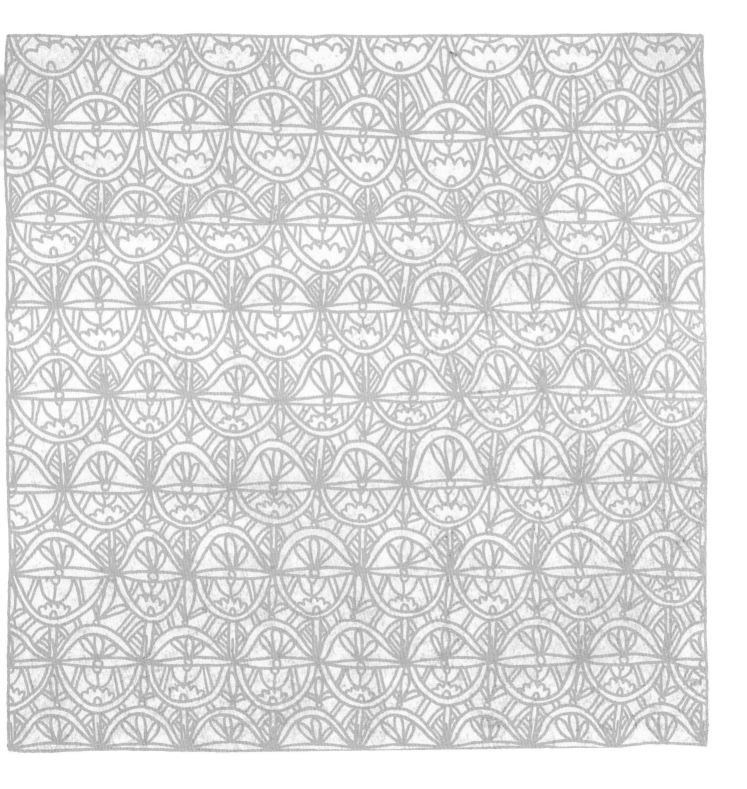

90464532R00029

Made in the USA
Middletown, DE
23 September 2018